ADVENTURE WITH PIGGY

A Day at the Beach: A Lesson on the Importance of Family

by Wendy Westerfield

Dream Big!

♡ Wendy Westerfield

WestBow Press books may be ordered through booksellers or by contacting:

WestBow Press
A Division of Thomas Nelson & Zondervan
1663 Liberty Drive
Bloomington, IN 47403
www.westbowpress.com
1 (866) 928-1240

Because of the dynamic nature of the Internet, any web addresses or links contained in this book may have changed since publication and may no longer be valid. The views expressed in this work are solely those of the author and do not necessarily reflect the views of the publisher, and the publisher hereby disclaims any responsibility for them.

Any people depicted in stock imagery provided by Thinkstock are models, and such images are being used for illustrative purposes only.
Certain stock imagery © Thinkstock.

ISBN: 978-1-5127-8617-0 (sc)
ISBN: 978-1-5127-8618-7 (e)

Library of Congress Control Number: 2017906893

Print information available on the last page.

WestBow Press rev. date: 5/30/2017

WestBow
PRESS®
A DIVISION OF THOMAS NELSON
& ZONDERVAN

A pig of good character, that's who Piggy is;
when he sees a need, he's the best in the biz.
He's ready to take a challenge you see,
teaching important values to every family.

Playing on his farm he waits for the bell to ring,
letting him know there's a family in need.

He wiggles his snout and away he goes,
where he'll end up nobody knows.

Peeking through the window to see why he's here,
he realizes his purpose; it all becomes clear.

Dad is on the computer, mom is on her phone,
brother is playing video games, and sisters are all alone.

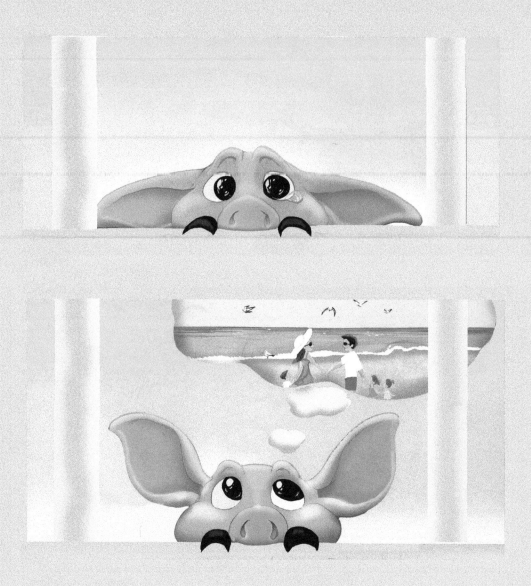

Piggy watches for a while, there is no communication.
Everyone's in their own world, they need a family vacation.
A time to be together without the world's distractions;
I think the beach would be a perfect plan of action.

There's a knock on the door, what do they see?
A cute little piggy smiling with glee.

Piggy sings, "I'm a Piggy who cares, a Piggy who sees,
when there is a family or person in need.
I've been watching your family closely you see,
and now won't you please take a journey with me?"

Dad looks and says, as Piggy wiggles his snout,
"Where are we going? What's this all about?"

The beach! It's beautiful, a great place to be—
the smells, the breeze, the sand, the sea.
There are families everywhere playing together—
laughing, talking, and spending time with each other.

Piggy looks at them and says, "What do you see?
Isn't this a picture of what a family should be?
How do you like to spend time with each other?
Take turns sharing– let's start with brother."

Brother says, "Oh my favorite is biking."
Dad says, "I like when we laugh and we sing."
Sister speaks up, "Playing at the park is the best."
Then Mom adds, "I like to cuddle and rest."

Our schedules are so full, there's no time to pause.
Our activities are fun, but I can see what they cause.
We're stressed and we're busy. We rush and we fuss.
We've lost what we love most: Our family, Our US.

We go here, we go there... always on the run.
And once we get home, there's more to be done.
Cooking, cleaning, laundry too;
school work, baths, and bedtime. Whew!

We don't mean to lose focus, but we're out of touch
with the ones God gave us- those we love so much.

Piggy, Piggy how can we change?
Give up all we do? That would feel really strange.
Piggy's snout curled and he gave a small sigh,
"That's why I brought you here, that's why I stopped by.
Look around you, be quiet and sit for a bit.
Feel the sand, hear the waves. Don't give up! Don't quit!"

God gave you family to love and spend time with;
to laugh with and sometimes even to cry with.

Family is important and family does matter—
don't listen to all of the noises and chatter.
Take time daily to invest in each other,
be the best father, mother, sister and brother.

Go on family date nights or just stay home.
Order pizza, have a picnic, and turn off your phone!
Play a board game, take a walk,
or sit around and talk.

These days are so precious, They are ticking away.
Slow down; enjoy your family, laugh and play.

Thank you Piggy for reminding us
just how important it is to invest.

We've taken a journey; you've helped slow us down.
Piggy says, "Now, it's my turn to get out of town.
There's another family waiting in need."
They look at each other with a smile and agree.

Piggy wiggles his snout, in an instant he's gone;
and our family is singing a brand new song.

Now how about you? What's your family's song?
Is it old? Is it new? Is it short? Is it long?

Like dear Piggy says, "Don't give up, don't you quit!"
Your family's valuable, you have to admit.
Let little things go, I encourage you today,
put your family first, laugh and play.

Date Nights for the whole family:

1. Go for a walk and talk... halfway there start racing.
2. Play a game in the yard: Tag, Baseball, Football, Soccer.
3. Get on teams and put on a lip sync battle to your favorite songs (don't forget to add choreography).
4. Order in and play board games.
5. Try to eat dinner at home at least 3 times a week together at the table (get a jar and put questions in it, each night pull out a question and go around the table for everyone to answer).
6. Go riding in the car (turn the radio on and see who can name and sing the first song they hear), laugh, and have fun.
7. Have breakfast for dinner, put on music, dance in the kitchen while you cook together.
8. Blankets on the floor, order pizza, and watch a movie.
9. Go camping in your backyard, roast hotdogs, make s'mores (or campout in your living room).
10. Blind fold everyone except one person. Give each person a piece of paper. Have the person not blindfolded give directions on making a paper airplane. See the outcome! and laugh.

CPSIA information can be obtained
at www.ICGtesting.com
Printed in the USA
LVHW01s1911010218
564967LV00005B/6/P